My Sparkly New Boots

By Jenny Goebel

Illustrated by Taia Morley

A GOLDEN BOOK • NEW YORK

Text copyright © 2023 by Jenny Goebel
Cover and interior illustrations copyright © 2023 by Taia Morley
All rights reserved. Published in the United States by Golden Books, an imprint of
Random House Children's Books, a division of Penguin Random House LLC, 1745 Broadway,
New York, NY 10019. Golden Books, A Golden Book, A Little Golden Book, the G colophon,
and the distinctive gold spine are registered trademarks of Penguin Random House LLC.
rhcbooks.com
Educators and librarians, for a variety of teaching tools, visit us at RHTeachersLibrarians.com
Library of Congress Control Number: 2022931982
ISBN 978-0-593-42741-5 (trade) — ISBN 978-0-593-42742-2 (ebook)
Printed in the United States of America
10 9 8 7 6 5 4 3 2 1

Off to the store. It's time for new shoes.
Spinning, circling, how will I choose?

Sneakers are fun. . . .

Dress shoes are cute. . . .

Sizing, selecting, I slip on a boot.

In polka-dot boots, I'd be off in a dash.
Jumping, sloshing, I'd make a big splash.

In sturdy brown boots,
I'd wade through a creek.

Clomping, stomping,
I'd hike to the peak.

In fluffy white boots, I'd play in the snow.
Winging, zinging, I'd duck, then I'd throw.

In tall black boots, I'd sail stormy seas.
Arrr, me hearties, I'd do as I please.

In cowgirl boots, I'd yell, "Giddyup!"
Clipping, clopping, I'd win a gold cup.

In zippered boots, I'd trek through the sand.
Plodding, trotting, I'd see distant lands.

In silver boots, I'd aim for the stars.
Zipping, zooming, I'd land upon Mars.

In sparkly boots, I'd dance and I'd sing.
Shining, dazzling, I could do anything!

In my sparkly new boots, I dream and pretend.

In my sparkly new boots . . .
I make a new friend.